What not to say to a bisexual

THE ESSENTIAL POCKET GUIDE

WhatNotToSayToABisexual.com

@WhatNotToSayToABisexual

Copyright © 2022 by J. Talison

All rights reserved. This book may not be reproduced in whole or part, stored in a retrieval system, or transmitted in any form or by any means – electronic, mechanical, or other – without written permission from the author, except by a reviewer, who may quote brief passages in a review.

ISBN 978-1-7391218-0-8 (Print)

ISBN 978-1-7391218-1-5 (eBook)

ISBN 978-1-7391218-2-2 (Print)

We may disagree, and that's ok.

Sexuality is a very personal thing and each of us should have the freedom to choose to what extent it is part of our public identity. None of us should assume another person's sexuality and they should not assume ours.

This guide is about helping non-bisexuals and bisexuals alike have better conversations about attraction and identity. Only you will be able to tell which may be ok for interactions with a friend, family member, partner or other person who may or may not have told you they are bisexual.

The entries in this guide are based on numerous conversations with a wide range of people across multiple countries, ethnic backgrounds, and age groups who identify as bisexual, and their allies. It also draws on my own experience as someone who has been openly bisexual for decades.

Attraction to more than one gender is not new and this guide focuses on "*bisexuality*" as it is the term most easily recognised and has the longest history. Much of this guide also applies equally across more recent terms to describe attraction such as *omnisexual* (to all genders and sexualities equally), *pansexual* (regardless of sex or gender identity), and *polysexual* (multiple genders).

Where gender is used, such entries should be seen to apply to those of any gender or none.

Sexuality is not a choice but deciding who knows and the extent to which it forms part of anyone's public identity should be theirs to determine. Identifying as bisexual in private is no less valid than the most openly vocal bisexual - there is no right or wrong way to be bisexual.

We may not get everything right and could even have got some parts very wrong. Perspective can also change with time and so what is appropriate now may not always be so. There is no problem if you disagree with a particular part, or the entire thing, but all involved do ask that you do so with consideration for the feelings of others.

Advocating for something as personal as sexual identity means continually listening. All involved also welcome any constructive feedback and insights that may assist us in making future editions of this guide more accurate and helpful for bisexuals and non-bisexuals alike.

J. Talison

*For all those who cannot or do not want
to be open about their bisexuality*

"Bisexuality is…"

Short answer
There's no single definition

Longer answer
Bisexuality is a broad term that's generally, but not exclusively accepted as a sexual, romantic, and or emotional attraction to more than one gender, but how it's defined can vary among those who identify as bisexual and in the wider community.

#2

"I assumed you were straight/gay"

Short answer

It's better not to assume

Longer answer

A person's sexuality should only be part of their public identity if they want it to be. Unless someone has told you who they are attracted to, then it's best not to make assumptions based on who they've dated, how they present themselves, etc.

"People are not born bisexual"

Short answer
Sexuality isn't defined at birth

Longer answer
A person's sexuality develops throughout their life. There is no set time someone may become aware they're attracted to more than one gender or understand this may mean they are bisexual. There is also no set time or way for someone to accept their bisexuality, disclose it to others, or act upon it.

#4

"You should come out and be public about it"

Short answer

Making your sexuality public is a choice

Longer answer

A bisexual person doesn't need to have their sexuality as part of their public identity. Despite the value in having queer role models, it's their choice alone as to who knows. Even if they may have told you or someone else, that doesn't give you permission to tell others or use it to describe them.

"Were you always bisexual?"

Short answer
There's a difference between being and identifying

Longer answer
Someone may have always known they were bisexual, or they may have later come to know this. How and when they came to know, and then disclose it, will be unique to each individual. Even if they said "no" yesterday but now identify as bisexual, it doesn't make their bisexuality any less valid.

#6

"It's your choice"

Short answer
Sexuality is not a choice

Longer answer
Being bisexual isn't a choice but it is up to each individual to decide whether they accept who they are or not. They should have the freedom to choose to what extent others know the types and genders of people they are attracted to as being bisexual is their truth to tell.

"Not many people identify as bisexual"

Short answer

Being openly bisexual is easier now

Longer answer

Thanks to the progress achieved by older generations and increasing social acceptance, more people now feel comfortable being open about their bisexuality. Research shows that in some countries young people are now more likely to identify as bisexual than gay, with far fewer seeing themselves as straight.

"You weren't bi before"

Short answer
Listen to what they are saying today

Longer answer
Sexuality is a complicated thing and each of us will go on our own path of discovery and disclosure. That can mean someone may be selective of what they say and when. What a bisexual person is telling you now is more relevant and important than what you were told or understood before.

> *"You're being greedy and will never be satisfied"*

Short answer
That's not how attraction works

Longer answer
Just as a straight person isn't attracted to all people of the opposite sex, bisexual people are not attracted to everyone but will often have different types of people they are attracted to across multiple genders. Like anyone else, they will need to determine for themselves whether they feel satisfied.

#10

"Are you sure? How can you be sure?"

Short answer

It's not a thing disclosed lightly

Longer answer

For most people being open about their bisexuality isn't easy to do, especially at first. If someone tells you they identify as bisexual, then it's best to assume they have already given some serious consideration about to whom they're attracted, as well as their reason for confiding in you.

"You can't have it both ways"

Short answer
Sexuality is a spectrum

Longer answer
Often embedded in the idea someone is only ever gay or straight, this kind of statement makes the false assumption that there are just two options for sexual attraction and that a person can only like a single gender at a time. There are a wide range of ways we can feel and express attraction to others.

#12

"I see myself marrying a man / woman"

Short answer
That's nice for you

Longer answer
Some people know the type of person they want to marry, but many do not. Many are not even actively thinking about marriage. A social expectation of who you want to be with should not be held up to someone else as a standard they should also meet.

"You're only half gay"

Short answer

There's no such thing as half gay

Longer answer

Being gay and bisexual are not the same thing. While some people may describe themselves as bisexual as part of discovering who they are, it doesn't mean bisexuality is just a stop along the way to being gay. A bisexual may also find it easier in some situations to let others assume they're gay or straight rather than explain.

"You're not good looking enough to be bisexual"

Short answer

Beauty is not a sexual identity

Longer answer

How attractive or not you find someone doesn't diminish their sexuality, or their freedom to express it or have it as part of their public identity. Even by social beauty standards, there is no requirement to look a certain way to be bisexual.

"You're just confused"

Short answer
Having a label can bring clarity

Longer answer
Confusion is part of personal discovery which drives many people to seek out answers to who they are. But once someone feels they have found who they are and that being bisexual is part of that, then any confusion which led to it may usually be long gone or much reduced.

#16

"Bisexuality doesn't exist. People are either straight or gay"

Short answer
There are many types of sexuality

Longer answer
Some people feeling attraction to more than one gender is an observed fact supported by a wealth of lived experience (as well as a substantial and growing body of empirical research). Some people may wish bisexuality didn't exist, but such a position usually just reflects their values and preferred world view.

#17

"Bisexuals will always cheat. How can you be trusted?"

Short answer
Sexuality is not loyalty

Longer answer
Infidelity isn't determined by a person's sexuality and the mere fact someone is attracted to more than one gender doesn't make them any more or less likely to be unfaithful. Trust is a personal thing built between two people regardless of sexuality and it is for them to maintain and determine what could damage or break it.

"So, you'll sleep with anyone?"

Short answer
Bisexuals can be just as picky

Longer answer
Someone identifying as bisexual simply means they are attracted to more than one gender, but that doesn't mean they have a broad taste in men, women, or anything else. Just like anyone, a bisexual person may find many different people attractive or only a few.

"You think there are only two genders?"

Short answer
Bisexuality doesn't define gender

Longer answer
The definition of bisexuality does vary but at a basic level it is commonly understood to simply mean sexual attraction to more than one gender. It's not a declaration that there are only two genders or that gender identity is fixed at birth, these are separate concepts that can at times overlap.

#20

"You need to pick a side"

Short answer

You're assuming there are sides

Longer answer

While a simplified view of the world may have served a purpose over recent decades in the fight for recognition of the queer community, human sexuality is far more complicated than someone being either straight or gay. Being bisexual is a valid sexual identity in its own right.

"Bisexuals have double the dating options"

Short answer
Not necessarily, quite often the opposite

Longer answer
Being bisexual doesn't mean someone is attracted to everyone and there may only be certain types of people of any particular gender they feel attracted to. Not to mention the bisexuality-based exclusion often experienced from potential partners can also tend to reduce the number of dating options.

#22

"When were you last with a man / woman?"

Short answer

Bisexuality does not expire

Longer answer

A person's sexuality is defined by who they are attracted to, not who they've been physically intimate with in the past. While being with someone of the same or opposite gender can help some discover, affirm, or celebrate who they are, a bisexual does not need to disclose their dating or sexual history to be legitimate.

#23

"You're not queer enough"

Short answer
There is no queer threshold

Longer answer
While sexuality itself isn't a choice, deciding how much it's part of your public identity, how much it informs your physical appearance or determines how you behave in public or private is entirely up to each individual to decide for themselves.

"Dating someone of the same gender means you're gay"

Short answer
Partners don't define sexuality

Longer answer
Who someone is currently dating doesn't define their sexuality any more than what they are eating for lunch defines their favourite foods. A bisexual person may never be with or even date all of the genders they are attracted to, and they don't need to.

"You need to tell potential partners"

Short answer
Only if they want to tell them

Longer answer
Every relationship is different, and the people involved need to determine what they want or need to disclose and when. For some there can be a big difference between identifying as bisexual and being comfortable disclosing it, even to their partner.

"You're into threesomes then"

Short answer

No more than anyone else

Longer answer

Being bisexual or however else someone may identify doesn't mean they are more or less into a particular sexual activity or number of partners. Just because someone is attracted to more than one gender doesn't mean they want to have them at the same time.

#27

"Into toys? Are you a top or a bottom?"

Short answer

What you like is what you like

Longer answer

A person's sexuality may inform what they like doing physically, but it doesn't determine it. Intimate preferences can vary between different people and being bisexual doesn't automatically mean someone is more or less inclined towards a particular sexual activity.

"You don't look bisexual"

Short answer
There is no way to look bisexual

Longer answer
Some people express themselves in ways that could be described as openly queer but that doesn't define who they are attracted to. The same goes for those who choose not to express their sexuality through their appearance at all. Bisexuality doesn't define anyone's appearance.

"You don't act gay/bi"

Short answer
Attraction doesn't determine behaviour

Longer answer
While some people do consider their actions through the lens of their sexuality, many do not and it's unwise to attribute a particular type of behaviour to bisexuality or anything else. Despite many stereotypes, there is no way someone can simply move or speak that fully reveals their sexuality.

#30

"Have you been in a straight / gay relationship?"

Short answer

Relationships don't have sexualities

Longer answer

Sexual identity is held by people, not their relationships. We all sometimes use terms such as "gay couple" but these are best avoided unless you know both their sexual identities and that each is ok with being public about it. Being in or having been in a same or opposite sex relationship doesn't make someone any less bisexual.

"You were raised wrong"

Short answer
Parents don't define sexuality

Longer answer
How and where someone is raised may make them more open to identifying as bisexual, but many people can find it difficult discovering and coming to terms with who they are. It is simply not the case that every opinion around sexuality should be accepted as equally valid.

"Who do you prefer? Is it 50/50?"

Short answer
An even split is unlikely

Longer answer
Some of those who identify as bisexual do consider their attraction to be equal across genders, but most will typically find they are more attracted at any time to one or another. Sexual identity isn't based on keeping score and doesn't even require someone to have ever had sex — you can be bisexual and a virgin.

"You'll make your mind up eventually"

Short answer
They have, they're bisexual

Longer answer
If someone reveals to you that they consider themselves to be bisexual, then that is them making their mind up. While some people may identify as bisexual as part of their own journey towards discovering and accepting who they are, most bisexuals will not later identify as something else.

"All bisexuals are the same"

Short answer
Every bisexual is unique

Longer answer
There are some ways bisexuals are alike but there is far more that separates them as individuals and makes them part of any number of different communities. A bisexual may or may not be a Christian, a gamer, a bad cook, speak English, have a disability, or any number of other things.

"Does your partner know?"

Short answer
Disclosure can and does vary

Longer answer
Whether a partner understands someone's sexuality the same way you do is a matter for that person to discuss with their partner. There can be any number of reasons why those in a relationship may know more or less about the other person than you do.

"Bisexuality is a new thing"

Short answer
Bisexuality already existed

Longer answer
Increasing use of 'bisexuality', not least from more people feeling comfortable openly identifying as bisexual, may lead some to think it is a new concept. Attraction to more than one gender is something that has long been around in humans and other animals alike.

"You're not into monogamy then?"

Short answer
Relationship structures differ

Longer answer
Whether or not a relationship is exclusive, open, or somewhere in between is entirely the business of those within it and nobody else - just as the defining of boundaries and what is talked about is up to them. But none of that is unique to bisexuals.

#38

"Bisexuals are more promiscuous. You're addicted to sex"

Short answer

They want sex as much as anyone

Longer answer

Someone being attracted to more than one gender doesn't mean they will have or want sex any more than anyone else. Sex addiction is a real condition that requires professional care but identifying as bisexual doesn't mean someone is or will become addicted to sex or anything else.

"Do you have both a male AND female partner?"

Short answer
Relationship structures are separate

Longer answer
What partner(s) a person has and how they consider them a part of their life is determined by and within each relationship on their own terms. The sexuality of those involved doesn't determine if or how someone is another person's partner, but it can be a major influence.

"You're just doing it for the attention"

Short answer
There are easier ways to get attention

Longer answer
Someone wanting their bisexuality as part of their public identity may present it through things like their appearance, how they act, or what they want to talk about. But there are many more bisexuals who don't want it as a core or any part of their public identity.

"It's a phase. You're just experimenting"

Short answer
Sexual discovery is different

Longer answer
It is true that many people discover more about who they may or may not be through trying new things and experiences, including their sexuality. Experimenting is only part of bisexuality in that being with or better understanding others may help some bisexuals discover and confirm who they are.

#42

"You're more likely to get an STI/STD"

Short answer
That is simply not true

Longer answer
Sexual health risk is determined by the types of activities someone is involved in, the frequency with which they take part, and whether they have a proactive approach to testing and treatment. It has nothing to do with someone's sexuality.

"Only women can be bisexual"

Short answer
Bisexuals can be any gender or none

Longer answer
The limited representation of bisexuals in popular culture has mostly been through female fictional characters or musicians, leading many to assume women are more likely to be bisexual, or at least be open about it. A bisexual can be of any gender or none.

"Bisexual men are always on the dl / down low"

Short answer
Not being public is their choice

Longer answer
Many people don't like the idea of having their sexuality as part of their public identity, bisexuals included. Given the kinds of stigma still attached to any identity other than straight, there is little wonder some bisexual men choose to keep that part of their lives private.

#45

"You just haven't been with the right man or woman"

Short answer
Bisexuality isn't a waiting room

Longer answer
Sometimes you can meet someone and learn more about the world or yourself than you had ever known was possible. If someone has gone through the journey of realising and disclosing they are bisexual, then its best to believe them than think it's just temporary.

"Why do you need a label anyway?"

Short answer

Labels do help some people

Longer answer

There are lots of people who do not feel any need to give a name publicly or privately to their sexuality, including many that may otherwise be bisexual. But many others do find comfort in being able to easily describe that part of who they are.

"Biphobia isn't a real thing"

Short answer

It's real and does a lot of harm

Longer answer

People saying thoughtless and hurtful things or acting out because someone tells them they are bisexual is far too common, with many bisexuals experiencing more biphobia from within parts of the queer community than society more generally. Denying biphobia only makes it worse.

"All bisexuals are polyamorous"

Short answer
Types of relationship vary

Longer answer
Choosing to have more than one romantic relationship at a time isn't unique to people who identify as bisexual, and it is generally not the approach taken by most anyway. Just like everyone else, it's far more common to hear of bisexuals only wanting one relationship or partner at a time.

"You're scared of commitment"

Short answer
Interest in relationships differs

Longer answer
There is nothing about being attracted to more than one gender that makes someone who identifies as bisexual any more or less interested in commitment, having a relationship, or "settling down". They do however have to deal with all those who refuse to date a bisexual.

"Bi-erasure doesn't happen"

Short answer
It happens each and every day

Longer answer
Bi-erasure is the tendency by some to ignore or remove evidence of bisexuality. For example, only talking about the "gay community" can exclude other sexual and or gender identities from important discussions. Unless bisexuality is presented as a distinct identity, there is likely going to be some degree of bisexual erasure.

"Isn't everyone a little bisexual?"

Short answer
Sexuality is a spectrum

Longer answer
Most mainstream views place sexual attraction on a spectrum between exclusive heterosexuality and homosexuality. While there are different views, your place on the spectrum depends on things like awareness of who you are attracted to and your willingness to be open with others.

#52

"So, you're gay sometimes and straight other times?"

Short answer
It isn't a revolving door

Longer answer
Being bisexual doesn't mean someone is alternating between being attracted to people of the same then opposite gender, but to make things easier sometimes they may just call themselves straight or gay when the person or situation isn't worth the hassle.

"Prove it. Are you real bi or fake bi?"

Short answer
They don't have to prove anything

Longer answer
There is no way to prove any sexual identity and not accepting someone who identifies as bisexual based on some unscientific test is usually a reflection on the other person's values and experience. If someone wants to explain why they identify a certain way, then that is their choice, but you should not make or expect them to.

"Being bisexual is so trendy now"

Short answer

Sexuality is not a fashion choice

Longer answer

It's increasingly acceptable for people to openly identify as bisexual rather than the binary and absolute choice of being gay or straight, which can make it seem bisexuality is the latest thing people are doing to be or seem cool. Bisexuality isn't new, far from it.

"You'll eventually end up gay"

Short answer

It's only a halfway house for some

Longer answer

It was common in the past for gays and lesbians to identify as bisexual while discovering who they are and telling who they wanted to tell. Some may have sincerely felt they were bisexual while others may have described themselves that way due to other reasons, such as family pressure.

"You're lucky"

Short answer
Luck has nothing to do with it

Longer answer
In an ideal world sexuality would be a boring and mundane topic that brings no surprise and would only be known when someone chooses to have it as part of their public identity. If someone says "you're lucky", it can be good to make it known you're available to chat with them in case it's a hint that they may be struggling.

"I used to identify as bi"

Short answer
Everyone has a different journey

Longer answer
How and when someone identifies as bisexual is a personal thing that is unique to them, informed by their own experiences and preferences. Assuming someone will take the same path in discovering their sexuality as you can be harmful and should be avoided.

"That means you're easy"

Short answer

They are not more open to sex

Longer answer

Being bisexual doesn't determine how much or how little someone has had or wants to have sex, or who they have been with. Knowing someone identifies as bisexual is no way to determine how open they would be to doing anything sexual at any given time compared to any other kind of person.

#59

"You're too old to date, so it doesn't matter"

Short answer
Bisexuality has no age limit

Longer answer
Just as someone can come to realise they are bisexual quite young, there is no age when it is too late for you to realise who you are attracted to, come to terms with what this means, or disclose to others that you are attracted to people of more than one gender.

#60

"How do you know if you haven't had sex with a man / woman?"

Short answer
Sexuality is about attraction

Longer answer
Who you have or have not had sex with may inform how you understand who you are attracted to, but it doesn't determine who you are or your sexuality. Being bisexual is about whether someone is attracted to more than one gender, and not exclusively sexual attraction or sexual activity.

"You're not actually bi, you're just bi-curious"

Short answer
Bicurious is different to bisexual

Longer answer
Bicurious is a term often used by people still discovering their sexuality and those who don't wish to fully embrace the term bisexual for any given reason. As with anyone who discloses their sexual identity, the best approach is to accept what label they prefer.

"You're half normal"

Short answer

Queer people are just as normal

Longer answer

The idea of 'normal' has done a lot of harm in the world despite only being meaningful in the context of each person's own experience. Belief that queer people are not normal has been a key reason for so many losing friends and family connections after revealing their sexuality.

"That's so brave"

Short answer
Yes, it is brave

Longer answer
People who openly disclose their bisexuality often encounter a wide range of ignorant comments and hostile views from across society, but they don't just need to be told they are 'brave' for doing so. What they need are allies and proactive support from across the communities they are a part of.

"I couldn't date a bisexual"

Short answer
Then that's your loss

Longer answer
Sadly, too many bisexuals get told this kind of thing too often. But a person refusing to date someone who identifies as bisexual reveals both their ignorance and differing values, which can be better to know upfront than wasting time and finding out later.

Acknowledgment

Thank you to all of those who participated in the many discussions that helped to build each of the entries in this guide. Sharing your experiences has not always been easy but makes us all stronger.

Special thanks to Mutsa for helping brainstorm the initial idea and all your ongoing encouragement.

To those bisexuals and allies who volunteered to review various drafts of the guide, your time and commitment have truly been invaluable.

Creating something tangible would also not have been possible without the talent and expertise of all those who were part of the publishing process.

Finally, thank you to all those over the years who have made it OK for bisexual people like me to feel our sexuality is legitimate and created safe environments where we can choose to be open about it.

It's already clear this guide will create further discussions and I look forward to hearing even more experiences, understanding different points of view, and learning where we may improve in any future versions.

Thank you for reading.

www.ingramcontent.com/pod-product-compliance
Lightning Source LLC
LaVergne TN
LVHW051217070526
838200LV00063B/4936